TOO-IN-A-HURRY!

A Boy's Quest for an Arrow

Gail P. Scudder

Illustrated by Billy Thompson

To order additional copies of this book, contact:
Xlibris
1-888-795-4274
www.Xlibris.com
Orders@Xlibris.com

Illustrated by Billy Thompson

ISBN: Softcover   978-1-7960-4354-9
         EBook   978-1-7960-4353-2

Print information available on the last page

Rev. date: 10/09/2019

TOO-IN-A-HURRY!

A Boy's Quest for an Arrowhead

Seven-year-old Bobby Hillard woke up on a beautiful summer morning, looked out the window, and saw his neighbors, Charlie and Lester, getting ready to take their daily walk in the woods. Running circles around them was Charlie's little wire-haired terrier dog, Butchie, who couldn't wait to chase the little critters he would find along the trail.

Bobby sighed. "How I wish I could go with them!"

He heard his mother calling him to come for breakfast, so he put on his clothes, slid down the banister, jumped off, and headed for the kitchen where his mother was making his favorite breakfast— pancakes and bacon. Little did he know, as he hugged his mother good morning, that this day would bring many surprises for him.

Since the beginning of summer vacation, Bobby had been asking his mother if he could go hiking with "the boys," the nickname given to all the older men in town like Charlie and Lester, but her answer was always the same. "No, you are too young, and you will be in the way."

"But, Mom," he would beg, "how am I going to find my Indian arrowheads if you don't let me go?"

"Arrowheads, arrowheads—that's all you think about," she scolded.

It's true—ever since he and his mother moved to their little house in Portland, Pennsylvania, and he became friends with Charlie and Lester, he wanted to go on hikes with them to find arrowheads that were carved by the tribesmen of the American Lenape Indians, who lived along the Delaware River hundreds of years ago. But summer was coming to a close, and he wanted his arrowhead. He tried one more time.

"Mom," he said, "can I please, please go with—" But before he could finish what he was about to say, she interrupted him, smiled, and said, "Okay, but take along your jacket in case it gets chilly out there."

He bounded back up the stairs to his bedroom, shouting to his mother, "Tell them to wait, tell them to wait for me!" He grabbed his jacket, slid down the banister again, and was ready to go.

As he reached the kitchen, he could see Charlie and Lester walking toward his house. He couldn't believe that he was going into the woods to find his arrowhead. He gulped down his breakfast and headed toward the kitchen door to meet his friends, but first, he had to put his empty glass and plate into the kitchen sink and wipe his hands and face on a little towel his mother left out for him.

As he started for the door, his mother tapped him on the shoulder and said, "I have something special for you," and she reached into her pocket and pulled out a little leather drawstring pouch she had sewn for him.

"What's this for?" he asked.

"It's for you to carry your arrowhead home," she said.

"Do you really believe I'll find an arrowhead?" he asked.

"Yes, son, I do," she said, "but don't be too disappointed if you don't find one today."

"I know, Mom." But he still thought he would find one today.

He put the pouch in his jacket pocket, hugged his mother goodbye, and just as he opened the kitchen door to leave, he stopped and said, "Mom, how did they know to wait for me today?"

She just smiled at him and said with a warning, "Just be careful and behave," and he ran to meet his friends.

"Well, Too-in-a-Hurry, are you ready to go?" his friends asked when he opened the kitchen door.

Bobby laughed at the Indian name they had given him. "Yes!" Bobby answered.

Instead of calling his friends "the boys," he addressed them as Indian chiefs. "Mom, I'm leaving with Chief Charlie and Chief Lester." And away they went, with Butchie now circling the three of them.

Too-in-a-Hurry learned to love the Indians while spending many hours on the front porch of Lester's white clapboard house. Charlie would join them and, while eating cookies and drinking lemonade supplied by Bobby's mother, talk about the Lenape-Delaware Indian Tribe that lived along the Delaware River.

The boys told Bobby many stories about how the Indians hunted for deer and rabbits for food, planted corn, and other good things to eat. They talked about the beautiful horses they rode without saddles; the tents they lived in; the way they painted their faces for decoration, hunting, or war; and the dances and drums they used to tell stories of Indian life.

Many nights Bobby would dream of being an Indian, and sometimes his mother would let him sleep outside in a little tent that the boys made, but if it started to rain, his mother brought him back into the house even though he wanted to stay in the tent and listen to the raindrops bouncing off the canvas.

All summer and after he did his homework during the school year, Bobby would read about all the Indian tribes living in the American wilderness and how they cooked over fires and made beads, moccasins, and headdresses that they wore and sometimes sold. Some even lived in caves hidden in the mountains.

Sometimes Bobby had dreams about an Indian chief smiling down on him and handing him an arrowhead. He loved that dream because it seemed so real.

And now, for the first time in his little life, he was actually walking in the woods to hunt for arrowheads. As they walked the trails along the Delaware River, Charlie pointed out different flowers and trees and the way to tell the difference between an oak tree and an elm tree and even the maple tree, which is where the syrup that you pour on pancakes comes from.

Charlie pointed out more trees and plants to Bobby. "This is a Jack-in-the-pulpit. The plant had a long stem and a hood over it, and it is beautiful to see."

He also showed Bobby a little tree that has a small apple-shaped fruit that he picks and makes jam with. Bobby wanted to know if he could help Charlie make the jam, and he said, "Yes, when the fruit was ripe."

"Wait 'til I tell my mom," Bobby said excitedly.

Charlie also pointed out another plant that was nearby to Bobby. "This is poison ivy, and if you touch it, it will make you very itchy, and you will get red spots or a rash wherever it touches your skin."

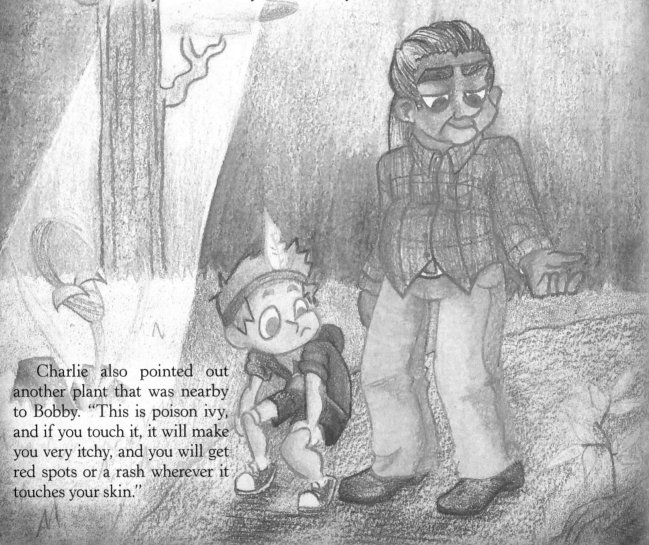

About ten minutes into their walk, they heard a train whistle blowing, and they headed toward the railroad tracks that stretched along the path close to the river. The screaming whistle got louder and louder, and they began to run faster and faster toward the tracks. The boys were huffing and puffing, and Bobby was laughing and yelling, as the train came thundering through.

They began pumping their arms in the air to signal the engineer to blow the whistle again and again, and Bobby kept jumping up and down as the cars went clickety-clacking, screeching, and rocking back and forth. They counted seventy-five cars before they saw the trainman in the caboose, the last car on a train, and they waved goodbye until the train disappeared with smoke puffing out of its stacks.

All the while, Butchie, who didn't like all the noise, was hiding behind a big tree and kept peeking out and barking until the train was gone.

Excited from all the fun, Bobby yelled out to his friends, "I am having the best time of my life!" And he couldn't stop grinning as they both laughed and smiled along with him.

Charlie and Lester looked at each other and were happy that young Bobby was part of their hike today. He brought all the joy only young people know when they experience beautiful things in life that they never saw except in books or games. Real life was so much better than watching a video games on his cell phone, Bobby thought.

Back on the trail, they continued on their early morning walk and were surprised by several deer running past them.

At one point, Charlie stopped abruptly and pointed skyward, spotting a beautiful American bald eagle as it swooped down quickly into the water and came up with a big trout in its talons. They continued to watch as the bald eagle—America's symbol of strength, beauty, and majesty—continued flying down the river until it disappeared. Bobby had never seen an eagle in flight. He was so excited, especially to see it catch its own breakfast. He also felt a little sad for the poor fish that would be eaten, but he learned in school how nature supplies its own food since animals can't go to the supermarket, like his mother does every day. Even Butchie, who was busy chasing little critters, stopped to look at the eagle and barked a few times and then went back to chasing butterflies.

After having walked about a mile into the woods, they decided to stop at a little waterfall to enjoy the lunch Bobby's mother made for their outing.

Sitting together on big boulders that surrounded the waterfall, the men started to tell stories about their lives. Lester talked about his time as a Seabee in the United States Navy in the Pacific during World War II. His job was to help clear woods and forests and then build landing zones for airplanes and roads for tanks and trucks for the soldiers who were on the firing line. The airplanes needed a place to land, refuel, or have repairs made, while the infantry soldiers were able to move faster once the Seabees cleared paths through the woods and fields for the trucks to carry men and supplies like ammunition for the soldiers.

Charlie told of how he got into mischief as a boy. He was riding his bike on the way home one night, when he saw that someone had planted a lot of flowers in front of the town's only bank building. He pulled up all the flowers, but a police officer was standing across the street in the dark and saw him. He took the boy to the police station and called Charlie's parents to come take him home. His parents had to pay for the flowers, and Charlie had to go to the local nursery and buy more flowers and plant them at the bank. They also wouldn't allow him to ride his bike for a whole month. He learned a good lesson that day, he told Lester and Bobby, who thought the story was very funny.

After they finished their lunch and made sure they left the grounds around the waterfall as clean as they found it, the three hikers went back on the trail to the farmer's fields at the edge of the woods. That's where Bobby would be able to search for what he came for—arrowheads.

The recently plowed fields were perfect for finding arrowheads, and Lester took Too-in-a-Hurry to one of the fields and told him to look down while he was walking and pick up any stone that was black in color and shiny. It could just be a little piece of stone, but that could mean that it was a piece chipped off a bigger one the Indian was carving, which might be nearby.

After walking through several rows and finding little pieces of flint, Bobby set out on his own, now knowing what to look for. He took out his little pouch his mother made for him and hung it around his neck and headed for the next row in the field.

Bobby was getting very excited and started to walk, but Lester told him he was walking a little too fast.

"Take your time," Lester told him, "and bend down closer to the ground so you can see better."

Lester found a broken branch from a tree and gave it to Bobby to poke at the loose dirt as he walked, in case an arrowhead was near the top of the soil.

After about twenty minutes, with Lester and Charlie watching him from afar, Bobby began to see that his search would not be an easy one and that he needed to have patience. If he rushed through everything, he might miss seeing an arrowhead. He kept poking at the soil with his stick, moving stones over, and pushing others away, but he only came up with more dirt.

He wanted to stop, but he could see Charlie and Lester watching him, and their belief in him gave him strength to keep going. He started counting the rows—one, two, three, four—and found nothing. He turned at the end of the fourth row and saw a shiny piece of stone. He picked it up, but it wasn't a flint stone, so he threw it down. A few more rows with nothing and he began to feel the hot sun on his arms and face. Bobby stopped to take a few sips of water from his Boy Scout canteen but then kept going; after all, today could be his only chance to find an arrowhead. But after looking for his treasure for almost an hour, he began to get tired and felt disappointed.

"I'll never find an arrowhead," he cried. "I don't know how to do it!"

He kicked up some dirt.

He then decided he would rest in the shade of an old oak tree. He sat down and leaned his head against the tree and rested for a few minutes, just as an Indian may have done so many years ago.

Then he saw the Indian Chief Nomad from his dreams who always gave him an arrowhead, and he blurted out to the Indian chief, "I can't find an arrowhead, I don't know how."

The chief smiled at him like he always did, but this time he didn't give Bobby an arrowhead but told him to pick the pink flower for his mother. Bobby didn't know what flower he was talking about, but before he could ask the Indian chief, he disappeared.

Feeling disappointed and sad now, Too-in-a-Hurry started to get up to look for Charlie and Lester so he could go home. As he stood up, he noticed a little flower near his right hand. He wondered if that's the pink flower the Indian chief told him about, and since he didn't find his arrowhead, he thought he would pick the pink flower and bring it to his mother in the little pouch she made for him. He remembered what she had told him about not being too disappointed if he didn't find an arrowhead, but he couldn't help it, he was disappointed. Bobby started to dig around the flower so he could get to the roots, when his thumb hit something very sharp. He pulled his hand back quickly because he thought he cut himself, but as he was cleaning the flower stem to put it in his new pouch, he noticed a black pointy stone stuck to the flower. He went to push it away and then stopped. He looked closer and closer at the little stone and began to realize that what he was holding in his hand and brushing away was what he was looking for all along, even from before he left his house, even before he ever knew Lester and Charlie.

IT WAS AN ARROWHEAD.

He jumped up and started screaming and yelling, "I found one! I found one! I found one!"

Charlie and Lester could hear him yelling from across the field and saw him running toward them with something in his hand, and as he got closer, they saw it was a pink flower. They wondered why he was so excited about a flower. But the closer he got to them, they realized he was shouting, "Arrowhead! Arrowhead!" And they too began excitedly waving back at him. After they did an Indian dance, whooping and hollering to celebrate Bobby's arrowhead, they asked him how he found it, and he said, "I didn't find it. The Indian chief found it for me."

"What Indian chief?" they asked.

"Indian Chief Nomad," Bobby said. "He always comes to me in my dreams, but today he was here and told me to pick the pink flower for my mother, and the arrowhead was under the flower!"

Charlie and Lester looked at each other, laughed, and then turned to Bobby and said, "You have been out in the sun too long, let's go home,"

Charlie whistled for Butchie, and then they headed home, Bobby, smiling to himself and clutching tightly his two prized possessions: a flower for his mother and his favorite thing in all the world, an arrowhead. He wasn't as tired now or feeling sad, and he couldn't wait to show his mother what he found.

When they finally reached home, he started calling to her, "Mom, Mom, come see my arrowhead! And guess what? Charlie and Lester invited me to have breakfast with all the boys in the woods!"

Tears came to his mother's eyes, and she hugged Charlie and Lester and thanked them for finding the arrowhead for him.

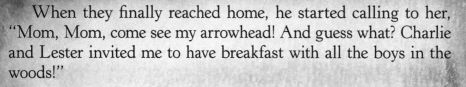

"We didn't find the arrowhead, your son said his friend, the Indian chief, did," Lester said.

"Oh, he's always telling me about that Indian chief, but I just humor him," she told the boys.

But Bobby knew the truth and held on to his treasure and just smiled.

CPSIA information can be obtained
at www.ICGtesting.com
Printed in the USA
BVHW021202181019
561474BV00002B/30/P

9 781796 043549